I Hug

David McPhail

I Like to Read®

HOLIDAY HOUSE • NEW YORK

I Like to Read® books, created by award-winning
picture book artists as well as talented newcomers,
instill confidence and the joy of reading in new readers.

We want to hear every new reader say, "I like to read!"

Visit our website for flashcards and activities:
www.holidayhouse.com/I-Like-to-Read/
#ILTR
**This book has been tested by an educational expert
and determined to be a guided reading level A.**

I LIKE TO READ is a registered trademark of Holiday House, Inc.

Copyright © 2017 by David McPhail
All Rights Reserved
HOLIDAY HOUSE is registered in the U.S. Patent and Trademark Office.
Printed and bound in March 2017 at
Tien Wah Press, Johor Bahru, Johor, Malaysia.
The artwork was created with watercolor
over pen and ink on illustration board.
www.holidayhouse.com
First Edition
1 3 5 7 9 10 8 6 4 2

Library of Congress Cataloging-in-Publication
Data is available.
ISBN 978-0-8234-3854-9 (hardcover)
ISBN 978-0-8234-3847-1 (paperback)

To Zabella and her parents,

Merneah and Jamie

I hug my cat.

I hug my dog.

I hug my fish.

I hug my rock.

I hug my tree.

I hug my friend.

I hug my dad.

I hug my mom.

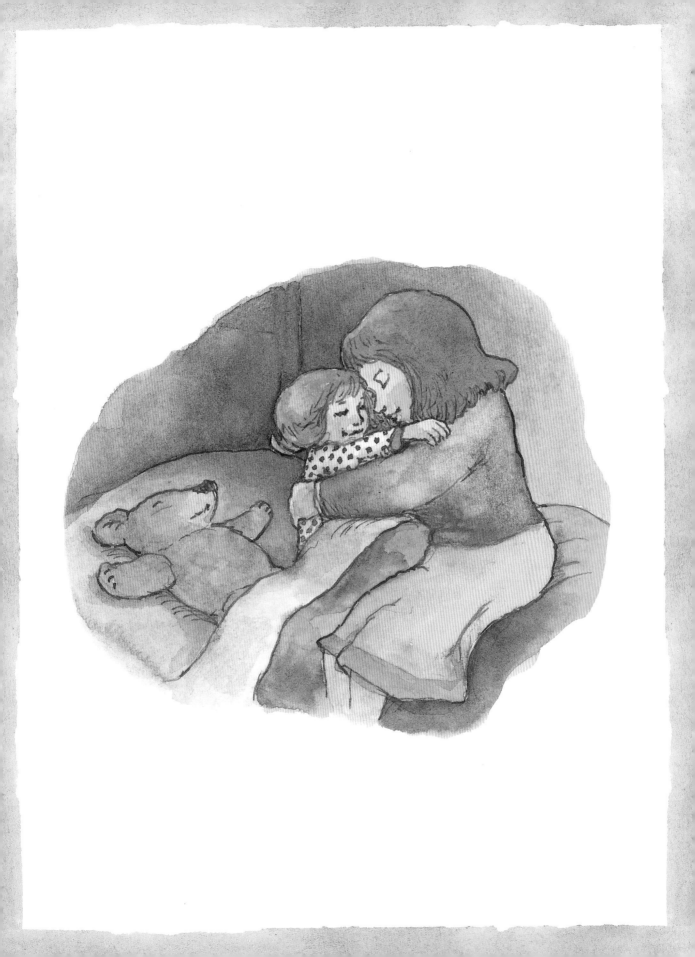

I hug my bear.

I hug my pillow.

I hug.